Sam,

Happy 4th Birthday.

love, Auntie Sarah &
Uncle Cookie
xxx

lauren child

I will not ever NEVER eat a tomato

featuring Charlie and Lola

ORCHARD BOOKS

This book is for Soren

who is crazy about tomatoes

but would never eat a baked bean

with love from Lauren

who is keen on Marmite

but would rather not eat a raisin

Orchard Books, 96 Leonard Street, London EC2A 4XD

Orchard Books Australia, 31/56 O'Riordan Street, Alexandria, NSW 2015

Text and illustrations © Lauren Child 2000

First published in Great Britain in 2000

ISBN 1 84121 397 7 (hb)

The right of Lauren Child to be identified as the author and the illustrator of this work

First paperback publication in 2001

ISBN 1 84121 602 X (pb)

has been asserted by her in accordance with the Copyright, Designs and Patents Act, 1988.

A CIP catalogue record for this book is available from the British Library

Printed in Singapore

2 3 4 5 6 7 8 9 10 (hb)   3 4 5 6 7 8 9 10 (pb)

I have this little sister Lola.
        She is small and very funny.
    Sometimes I have to keep an eye on her.
Sometimes Mum and Dad ask me to give her her dinner.
    This is a hard job because she is a very fussy eater.

Lola won't eat carrots, of course.
She says carrots are for rabbits.

I say, "What about peas?"

Lola says,
"Peas are too small
and too green."
One day I played a good trick on her.

She was sitting at the table
waiting for her dinner.
And Lola said,
"I do not eat

Peas or carrots or potatoes

or Mushrooms or spaghetti

or eggs or

sausages.

I do not eat

cauliflower or cabbage or baked beans

or bananas or oranges.

And I am not keen on

apples or rice or cheese

or

fish fingers.

And

I absolutely

will not ever

never

eat a tomato." (My sister hates tomatoes.)

And I said,
"That is lucky

because we are not having any of those things.

We are not going to eat any peas or carrots
or potatoes or mushrooms or spaghetti or eggs or sausages.

There will be no cauliflower or
cabbage or baked beans or bananas or oranges.

Lola looks at the table.

"But why are those Carrots there, Charlie?

And I said,
"Oh you think these are carrots.
These are not carrots.
These are orange twiglets from Jupiter."

"They look just like carrots to me," says Lola.
"But how can they be carrots," I say.
"Carrots don't grow on Jupiter."

"That's true," says Lola.
"Well I might just try one
if they're all the way from Jupiter.
Mmm, not bad," she says, taking another bite.

Then Lola sees some peas.

"I don't eat peas,"

says Lola.

I say,

"These are not peas,

of course they are not,

these are green drops

from Greenland.

They are made

out of green

and fall from the sky."

"But I don't eat green

things," Lola says.

"Well maybe I'll nibble just one or two. Oh," says Lola, "quite tasty."

Next Lola spies the potato.
"I will not eat potato
so don't even try,
not even mash."

"Oh,
this
isn't mash.
People often
think that but no,
this is cloud fluff from
the pointiest peak of Mount Fuji."
"Oh well, in that case a large helping for me;
I love to eat cloud."

"Charlie,"
she says,
"they look like fish fingers to me,
and I would
never
eat a fish finger."

"Oh, I've been to that supermarket,
one time with Mum.
Yes, I know the ones.
I think I've had them before," Lola says, gobbling.
"Are there any more?"

And then Lola says,

"Charlie will you pass me one of those?"

And I say,

"What, one of those?"

And Lola says,
       "Yes, Charlie,
one of those."
       And I can't believe my eyes
because guess what she is pointing at,
the **tomatoes**.

And I say,

"Are you sure?

Really?

One

of these?"

And she says,

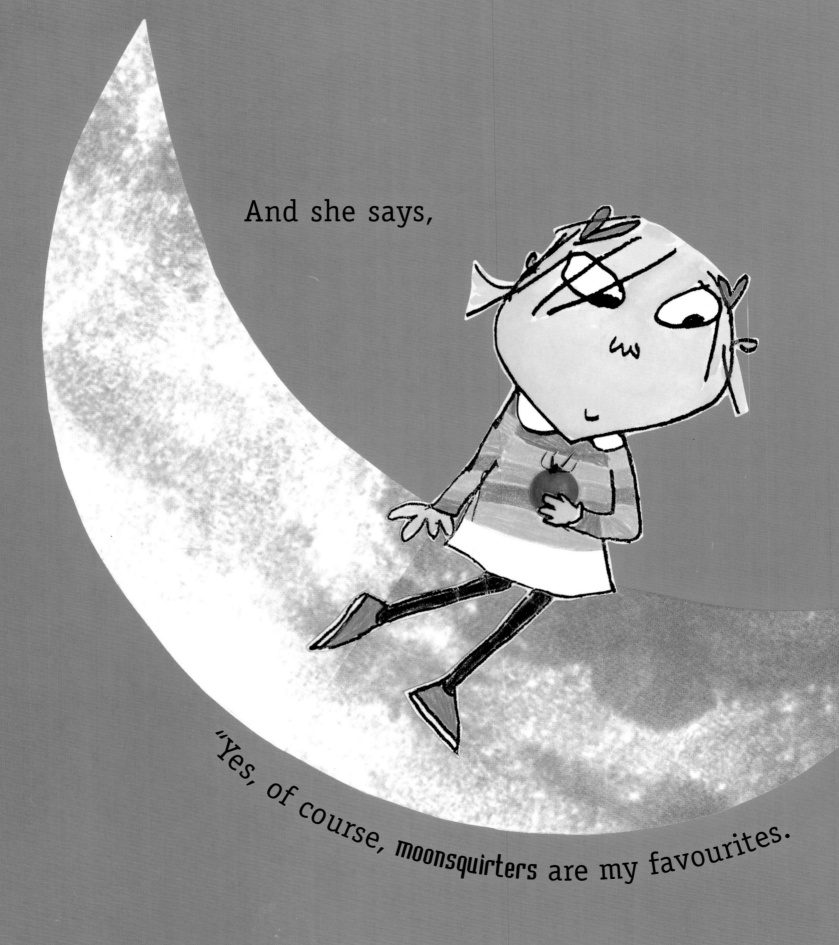

"Yes, of course, moonsquirters are my favourites.

Charlie

"You didn't think they were toMatoes,
did you, Charlie?"